WE LOVE SCHOOL!

Marilyn Janovitz

NorthSouth

New York / London

We like our garden.

We like our pet.

We like saying the alphabet.

We like to cut.

We like to glue.

We like to hang the art we do.

We like to swing.

We like to slide.

We like lining up to go inside.

We like snack time, and we know

we need good food to help us grow.

We like to sing. We like to clap.

We like to take a little nap.

We like to stretch. We like to bend.

We like sharing with a friend.

We like to measure. We like to weigh.

We like dressing up to play.

We like to count. We like to spell.

We like having show-and-tell.

We like paint. We like clay.

We like putting things away.

We like learning something new.

Oh, we LOVE school—

and our teacher, too!

All rights reserved. No part of this book may be reproduced or utilized in any form or
by any means, electronic or mechanical, including photocopying, recording, or any
information storage and retrieval system, without permission in writing from the publisher.

First published in the United States, Great Britain, Canada, Australia, and New Zealand in
2007 by North-South Books Inc., an imprint of NordSüd Verlag AG, Zürich, Switzerland.
Distributed in the United States by North-South Books Inc., New York.

Library of Congress Cataloging-in-Publication Data is available.
A CIP catalogue record for this book is available from The British Library.

ISBN: 978-0-7358-2112-5 (trade edition)
10 9 8 7 6 5 4 3 2

Printed in Malaysia